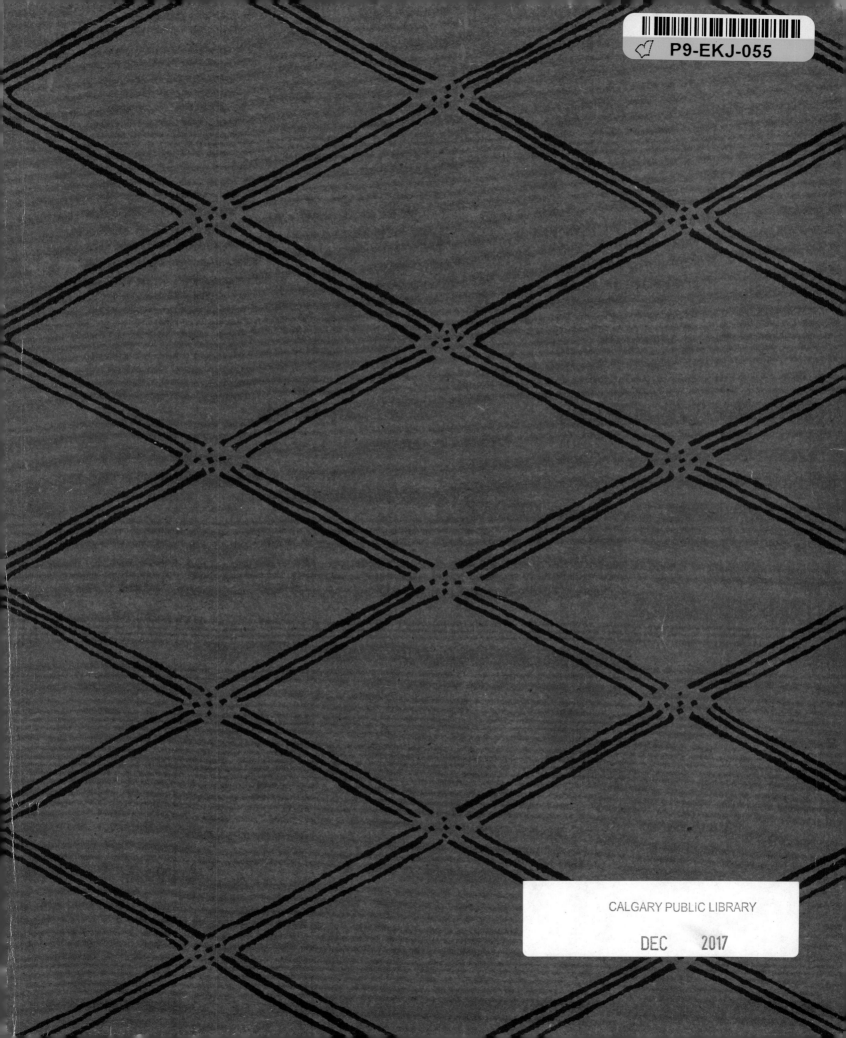

CHOCOLATE
CAKE
MICHAEL
ROSEN

KEVIN
WALDRON

PUFFIN

For Emma, Elsie & Emile – M.R.

For Ben – K.W.

PUFFIN BOOKS

UK | USA | Canada | Ireland | Australia | India | New Zealand | South Africa
Puffin Books is part of the Penguin Random House group of companies whose
addresses can be found at global.penguinrandomhouse.com.

Penguin
Random House
UK

First published 2017
001

Printed in China
A CIP catalogue record for this book is available from the British Library

ISBN: 978–0–141–37409–3

All correspondence to: Puffin Books, Penguin Random House Children's
80 Strand, London WC2R 0RL

When I was a boy,
I had a favourite treat.
It was when my mum made . . .

chocolate cake!

ohhh! I LOVED chocolate cake.

My mum, she says to me,
"Listen, Michael,
if there's any chocolate cake
left over at the end of the day,
you can take some to school
tomorrow to have at play time
or at lunch time."

So I used to go to school
with a piece of chocolate cake
in my little box.
And I'd be walking to school . . .

Yeahhh!
It's in there.
I know it is.

And I'd get to school,
and it would be play time or lunch time
and I'd open up the box,
take it out . . .

Open up the paper . . .

I LOVED my mum's chocolate cake.

And one time,
there WAS some chocolate cake
left over at the end of the day.
And I went to bed
and I was fast asleep,
and then,
in the middle of the night . . .

I woke up!

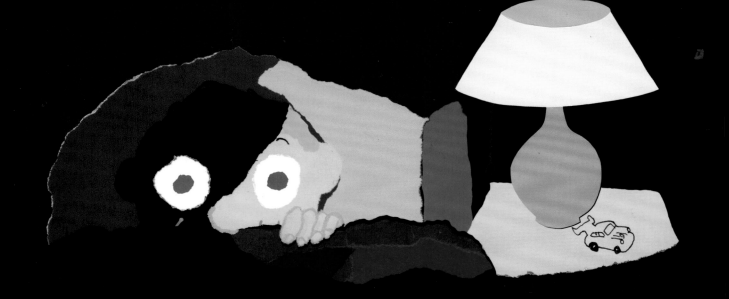

And I thought

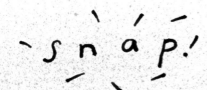

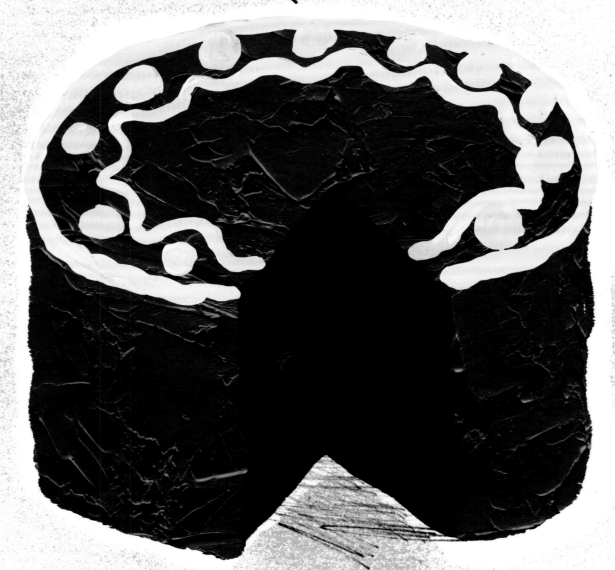

chocolate cake!!!

Heh-heh!

Maybe I could go downstairs
and have a little look at it.

No one would know.

So I got up out of the bed . . .

Along the passage . . .

Careful not to tread on the creaky floorboard
outside Mum and Dad's bedroom,
because if they wake up and find me
I'll be in BIG TROUBLE.
So, really quiet.

Are they still asleep? Yes. OK.

Along the passage . . .

down the stairs . . .

into the kitchen . . .

open the cupboard . . .

and . . .

Yeahhh!
There
it is!!!

And then I notice some little crumbs on the plate. So I think, if I lick the end of my finger, I could pick up some of those crumbs and no one would know anything about it.

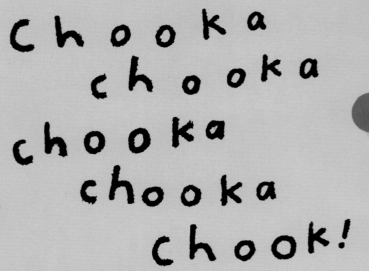

Oh yeahhh!
Little sticky bit there.

And then I notice
on the side of the cake
there's some little crumbly
bits just falling off.
So I think,
if I take a knife
I could just ...

Scrunch-it-all-together-
and-there's-the-crumbly-bits-
and-the-sticky-bits-
and-it's-all-gonna-go-in-there-
yeah-belly-belly-belly!

OOOmmmm-myom-yom-

OOOOMMMM!!!

Gobble!

Mmmm.

... tidy it up a little bit.
No one would notice.

SCRRRAPE!
SCRRRRAPE!

And then I notice that as I've tidied
it up a little bit over here,
then maybe I could just
even it up a bit over here.

So I take the knife again
and this time . . .
THROUGH the crispy icing
on the top . . .
THROUGH the squashy icing
in the middle.

SCRRRRAPE!

And I've got a whole slice this time —
yeahhhh!
And it's all gonna go in there.

It's a . . .
belly-belly-belly.
And it's . . .

And now
I've got the taste of it in my mouth
and I can't stop myself,
so I go

Ya-Pshhh!
Ya-Pshhh!

And I've got these slices,
so I go

Gobble!
Gulp!
Gobble!
Gulp!
Gobble!
GULP!
Gobble!
GulpGulp!

I can't stop myself . . .

Greedy!

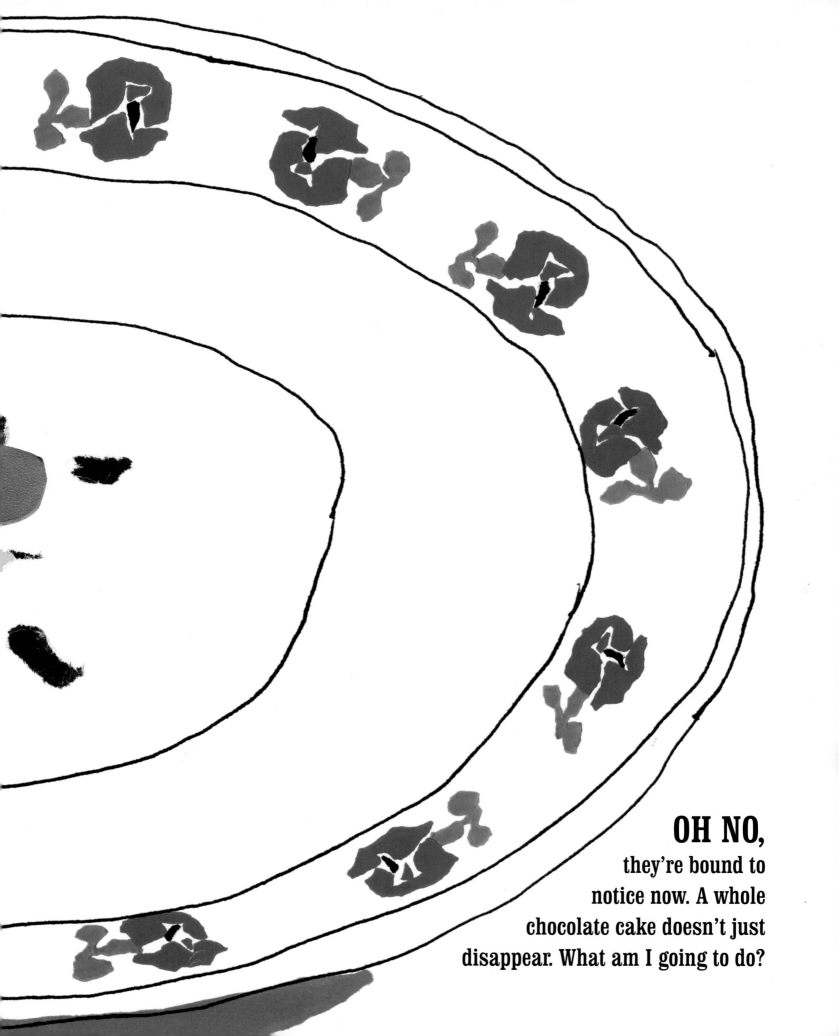

OH NO,
they're bound to
notice now. A whole
chocolate cake doesn't just
disappear. What am I going to do?

And don't forget to dry up.
Get the cloth.
And don't forget the knife.

And don't forget to put
them away. Plate
— in the cupboard.

And the knife —
in the drawer.

And back up to bed: shhhh!

Up the stairs . . .

Along the passage . . .
I know where the creaky floorboard is now.
So, all I've got to do is tread OVER it,
because if I tread ON it, and it makes a noise,
I am DEAD!

Are they still asleep? Yes. It's OK.
Into the bedroom . . .
into bed . . .
under the covers . . .

Aaah. Nice warm feeling:
chocolate cake in my belly,
goody, goody, goody.
And I go to sleep.

In the morning

I get up

and I go downstairs.

And I'm having my breakfast.

And Mum is busy over there

and she's busy over there . . .

And then she says,
"Oh! Michael, don't forget
your book folder."
She hands me my book folder,
and I'm busy having
my breakfast.

She's busy over there ...

she's busy over there.

And then she says,
"Oh! Michael!
There's something else:
there's something nice,
there's some chocolate cake
left over from yesterday
for you to take to school today."

And I went,

...all right.
Yeah.

And she says, "What's the matter? You usually jump at the idea of having chocolate cake."

And I went,

Yeah, it's all right... it's OK.

CORN

And she's looking at me very closely,
just here, next to my mouth.
And she says, "What's that?"

And I said, "What's what?"

"It's not . . . chocolate cake, is it?"

And I said,

And she went over to the cupboard.

"IT'S GONE!
THE CHOCOLATE
CAKE'S GONE!!!

You haven't eaten the WHOLE
of the rest of the chocolate cake,
have you?"

And I said,

"You **don't know?**" she said. "You **don't know?**
I don't believe a word of it . . .
Now, off you go to school . . .

...NO!
Before you go to school,
go upstairs to the bathroom,
and wash your
dirty,
sticky face!"

I went upstairs to the bathroom,
and I looked in the mirror.

And I saw it —
just there:

chocolate **smudge!**
chocolate **blob!**

And I looked at it
and I thought, maybe,
next time we have
chocolate cake,
she'll forget about it.